This Ladybird Book belongs to:

All children have a great ambition … to read by themselves.

Through traditional and popular stories, each title in the **Read It Yourself** series introduces children to the most commonly used words in the English language (*Key Words*), plus additional words necessary to tell the story.
The additional words appearing in this book are listed below.

Heidi, aunt, Dete, mountains, grandfather, goats, sleep, hay, loft, happy, winter, grandmother, daughter, sick, miss, Clara, servant, dreamed, noises, ghost, wrote, doctor, carry, jealous, feet, worried, sorry, horrible, town, afternoon, taking, dream, dreaming, lived, helped, took, liked, living, called, having, walking, talked, waited, carried, carrying, putting, pushed

Ladybird books are widely available, but in case of difficulty may be ordered by post or telephone from:

Ladybird Books – Cash Sales Department
Littlegate Road Paignton Devon TQ3 3BE
Telephone 0803 554761

A catalogue record for this book is available from the British Library

Published by Ladybird Books Ltd Loughborough Leicestershire UK
Ladybird Books Inc Auburn Maine 04210 USA

Heidi

adapted by Fran Hunia
from the original story by Johanna Spyri
illustrated by Lynne Willey

Heidi had no mother or father.
She was looked after
by her aunt Dete.

One day Aunt Dete said,
"Come on, Heidi. We are
going up the mountain to see
your grandfather. You are going
to live with him as I have to go
to work in the town."

Heidi and Aunt Dete walked
up the mountain.

Peter was looking after
some goats on the mountain.

He took Heidi and Aunt Dete to
Grandfather's house.
Grandfather came out to see them.

Then Peter went home.

Soon Aunt Dete went back
down the mountain to work
in the town.

"Please take me into the house,
Grandfather," Heidi said.
"Where shall I sleep?"

Grandfather went up with her
to the hay loft.
"I like it up here," she said.
"Can I make my bed
in the hay?"

Grandfather helped her
and then they went down to eat.

Heidi went to sleep in her bed
in the hay loft.

The next day Peter came again.

"I am taking the goats up the mountain," Peter told Heidi. "Would you like to come with me?"

Heidi liked playing with Peter and she liked the mountain.

Then winter came. The goats had to stay in the goat house all day and Peter had to go to school.

One day Grandfather took Heidi
to see Peter's grandmother,
who could not see.

Heidi liked talking to her
and said that she would come
again soon.

Aunt Dete came to see
Grandfather.
"I have come to get Heidi,"
she said.
"I want to take her to the town."

"No," said Heidi.
"I like living here with Grandfather.
I don't want to go to the town."

But Aunt Dete said, "Come on, Heidi. Grandfather will be pleased to see you go, and you will like the town."

But Grandfather was very sad.

Aunt Dete took Heidi to see
a sick girl called Clara.

Heidi lived with Clara
and some servants.

Clara could not walk.
She had to sit in her chair all day.
So she was pleased to have
a friend to play with and talk to.

The servant who looked after
Clara didn't like Heidi.
"I will have to teach you
some manners," she said.

The servant talked on and on,
but it had been a long day
for Heidi.
She fell asleep in the chair!

The next day, Heidi looked
out of the window.
There were no trees or flowers.
All she could see were streets,
shops and houses.

"I don't like it here," said Heidi.
"I want to go home soon."

Then Clara's teacher came and the two girls had to do some school work.

That afternoon Heidi told Clara about her home on the mountain, about Grandfather, Peter and Grandmother.

Clara liked having a friend.

One day Clara's grandmother
came to stay. She liked Heidi
and was nice to her. Heidi liked
Clara and her grandmother,
but she was not happy
in the town.

Every night she dreamed
that she was at home
in the mountains.

One day the servants said that there had been noises in the nigh The next night one of the servants saw a white thing.

"Heidi!" said Grandfather.
"I am so pleased to have you
back!"

"It's good to be home,"
Heidi told him.

Soon Peter came down
the mountain with the goats.
He was pleased to see Heidi too.
They talked and talked.
Then Peter had to go home.

Heidi had some milk,
then she went up to bed
in the hay loft.
She didn't walk in her sleep
that night. She was so happy
to be home.

Every day Heidi went up
the mountain with Peter
and the goats.

Then one day Clara wrote
to say that she and
her grandmother were coming.

For two days Heidi didn't go
up the mountain with Peter.
She waited for her friends
to come.

Then she saw two men carrying Clara up the mountain in a chair. Grandmother was with her. Heidi was so pleased to see them!

Then Grandfather said, "Do you want to stay here with us, Clara?"

"Yes, please," said Clara.

"It will be good for her to stay
up here in the mountain,"
said her grandmother.

That night two happy girls went
to sleep in the hay loft.

The next day Peter came
to get the goats.
"Come on, Heidi," he said.

"I'm not going up the mountain,"
she told him. "I have
a friend here."

Peter went off with the goats
but he was jealous.

Heidi said to her grandfather,
"Can Clara go up the mountain
one day?"

"Yes," said Grandfather. "I will
push her up in her chair."

The next day Peter came to get
the goats. He saw Clara's chair
by the house. He was so jealous
that he pushed it down
the mountain and ran away!

Soon Heidi came out to get
the chair. It was not there. Heidi
and her grandfather looked
and looked for it, but they could
not find it.

"I will have to carry you up
the mountain, Clara,"
said Grandfather. He carried
her up and then went down
to look for her chair.

Clara and Heidi had
a happy day. Then Heidi went off
to look at some flowers.
"Wait here with Peter
and the goats, Clara," she said.

Heidi looked at the flowers.
"I would like Clara to see them,"
she said. She went back to Clara
and Peter.

"I want to take Clara to see the
flowers," she said. "You must
help me, please, Peter."

They tried to carry Clara,
but they could not do it.
Then Clara tried to help.

She put her feet down.
Then she said, "Look! I can walk!"
Heidi and Peter saw her walk
over to the flowers.

That afternoon Grandfather came
to get Clara. "Clara can walk!"
Heidi and Peter told him. Clara
walked a little way for him to see.

Every day Clara walked
a little more. Then they wrote
to Grandmother and asked her
to come. They didn't say
that Clara could walk.

When Grandmother came,
she saw that Clara
was not in her chair.

"What is going on?" she asked.

Then Clara walked
to her grandmother.
"How clever!" said Grandmother.

Clara and Heidi saw a man
coming up the mountain.
"It's Daddy!" shouted Clara.

Clara's father looked
at his daughter.
"Can this be my little Clara?"
he asked.

"Yes, Daddy," said Clara. "Look!"
And Clara walked to her father.
"You can walk!" he said.

"What a clever girl you are!"

Peter came down the mountain with the goats. He was worried.

"What is the boy so worried about?" asked Clara's grandmother.

"I know," said Grandfather. "Was it you who pushed Clara's chair down the mountain, Peter?"

"Yes," said Peter. "I'm very sorry. It was a horrible thing to do."

"Yes, it was," said Grandmother. "But some good has come of it. Clara can walk now, and we have to thank you for that. Now come on, Peter. We want to see your grandmother. Will you take us?"

"Yes," said Peter.
"She will be
pleased to see you."

And she was.

LADYBIRD
READING SCHEMES

Read It Yourself links with all Ladybird reading schemes and can be used with any other method of learning to read.

Say the Sounds

Ladybird's **Say the Sounds** graded reading scheme is a *phonics* scheme. It teaches children the sounds of individual letters and letter combinations, enabling them to tackle new words by building them up as a blend of smaller units.

There are 8 titles in this scheme:

1 **Rocket to the jungle**
2 **Frog and the lollipops**
3 **The go-cart race**
4 **Pirate's treasure**
5 **Humpty Dumpty and the ro**
6 **Flying saucer**
7 **Dinosaur rescue**
8 **The accident**

Support material available: Practice Books, Double Cassette pa
Flash Cards